Science of FOOD TREATS

Dear Reader

Everyone loves a food treat now and then – anything from whipped cream to jelly to fairy bread!
I thought it would be fun to investigate the science behind turning cream from a liquid into a fluffy consistency and what happens when jelly changes from a hot liquid into a wobbly solid.

ENJOY USING YOUR IMAGINATION TO "TASTE" THE TREATS IN THIS BOOK.

One of my favourite research tasks was investigating how hundreds and thousands are made – you can discover how this happens on pages 7–9.

I also enjoyed taking photographs of my friends, Kate and her mum, when they made choc-nut-chip cookies, jelly and whipped cream in my kitchen. The best job was tasting the results!

Enjoy!

Sharon Parsons

My sincere thanks to the following people for their time, information, images and enthusiasm for this book:

Stuart Walker, Carroll Industries NZ Ltd, Auckland, New Zealand

Karen and Kate Rafferty, Melbourne, Australia

The team at El Bulli, Roses, Spain

Contents

Science of FOOD TREATS

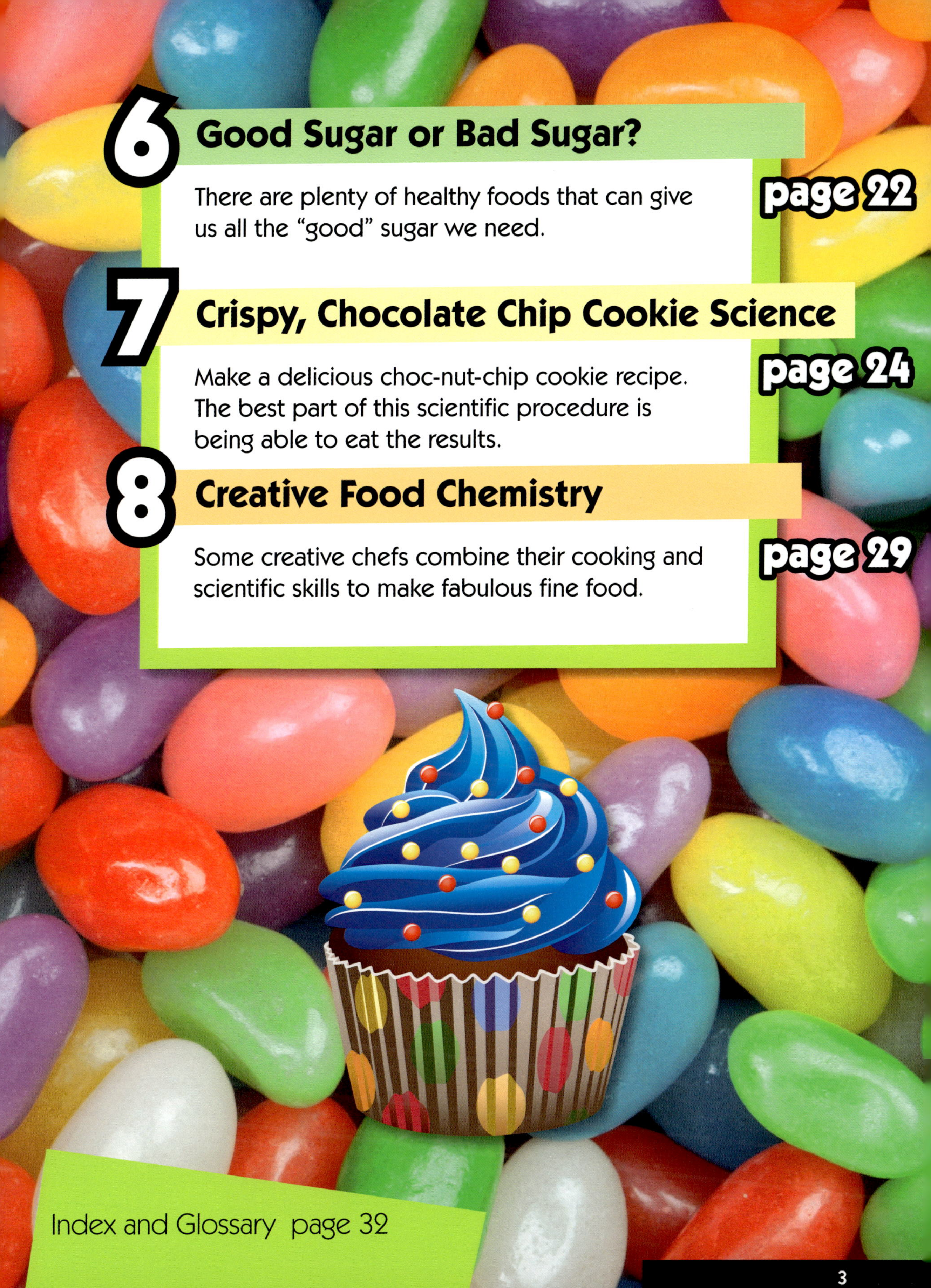

1 Food Treats

Cream, **Chocolate,** Jelly

Everyone should eat healthy food for most of the time … but sometimes we need to have smaller amounts of food treats. So while you're reading about whipped cream, jelly, chocolate chip cookies and hundreds and thousands on fairy bread, imagine their tastes in your mouth! Perhaps you have other favourite food treats that may include chocolate.

fun fairy bread

delicious whipped cream

wobbly jelly

Chocolate Treats

Most people love the taste of chocolate – it's so versatile because chocolate can be melted into liquid and also enjoyed as a solid.

One popular chocolate treat is to dip Spanish *churros* into warm melted chocolate.

Chocolate chips are usually made from compound chocolate.

Churros *are ready to be dipped into warm melted chocolate and enjoyed!*

ORIGIN OF *CHURROS*

Churros are Spanish doughnuts. They are made from a *churro* dough, which is piped through a *churrera* to form the traditional ridged shape. They are deep fried until crunchy on the outside, drained and sprinkled with sugar. Finally, they can be dipped in melted chocolate and enjoyed!

Is it Milk Chocolate or Compound Chocolate?

Milk chocolate is made from cocoa beans and milk solids. Processed cocoa beans provide cocoa solids and cocoa butter. The cocoa solids add flavour to the chocolate and the cocoa butter adds a smooth texture. The milk solids add a sweeter taste and a creamier texture.

Compound chocolate does not use cocoa butter. Vegetable oils are used instead, which makes the chocolate easier to melt and set. Many Easter eggs use compound chocolate. The vegetable oils affect the flavour of the compound chocolate.

Cocoa beans come from the seeds of the cacao plant.

a cross-section of a cacao pod

takeaway churros

A strawberry dipped in milk chocolate is delectable!

A chocolate fountain is fun!

Food Scientists

focused on microscopic work

Food Scientists

Food scientists usually work in laboratories where they study and test food and drinks in order to make them safer, tastier and more nutritious. Food production companies often employ food scientists to ensure that the food they produce is safe and nutritious when it is packaged.

Students who want to be food scientists must:

- study science subjects, such as chemistry and microbiology
- enjoy working with people
- want to work with all kinds of foods.

teamwork is important

2 Hundreds and Thousands Science

Almost no young kid's birthday party table is complete without a plate piled high with fairy bread. For over 200 years, hundreds and thousands have been sprinkled on bread, cakes and buns for decoration and fun.

NONPAREILS

In the food industry, hundreds and thousands are known as "nonpareils". The words "non pareil" are French for "nothing equal to". Their size varies from 1.2 to 1.5 millimetres in diameter. They are available in single colours and rainbow blends.

Who **Makes** Hundreds and Thousands?

Carroll Industries, in Auckland, New Zealand, is one of many companies around the world that make hundreds and thousands, and other sprinkles for baking decoration. The company shares their science secrets for making hundreds and thousands.

1. Get Ingredients

Raw ingredients are delivered to the warehouse: **starch** and **sugar**.

raw ingredients stacked in the warehouse

processing raw ingredients

Starch is made from maize.

Sugar is processed from sugar cane.

2. Mill Sugar

Sugar is milled in a **machine** to make a fine, powder-like icing sugar.

3. Mix Ingredients

A dry mix of the fine icing sugar, starch and special sugars is made in a large **blender**.

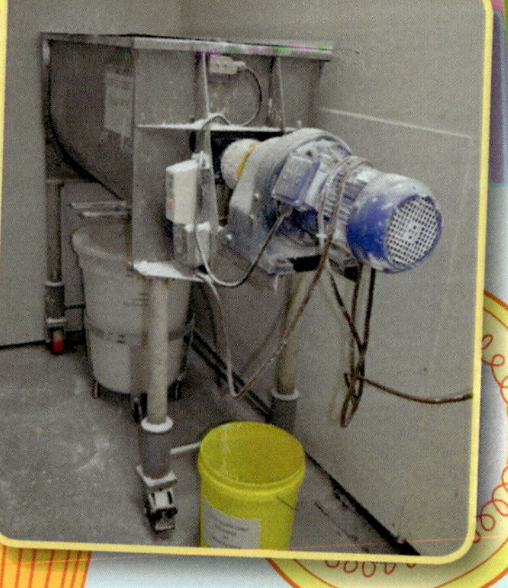

4. Coat Hundreds and Thousands

The dry mix coats the hundreds and thousands grains in large, heated **rotating pans** for up to three hours.

5. Sieve Hundreds and Thousands

The hundreds and thousands are **sieved** so that only those within the acceptable size range remain.

6. Sort Hundreds and Thousands

The remaining white hundreds and thousands are fed into a large **rotating pan**.

7. Colour Hundreds and Thousands

One **colour** is sprayed onto the white hundreds and thousands. Each batch of white hundreds and thousands is coloured separately.

a two-colour mix

8. Dry Hundreds and Thousands

Each batch of coloured hundreds and thousands is dried in a **heat room** or special dryer to remove any moisture.

Dried hundreds and thousands are **sieved** again to ensure they are even in size.

Batches of single-coloured hundreds and thousands are blended together in a large **rotating pan**.

Then the hundreds and thousands are ready to be weighed on **scales**, poured into bags and packed into **cartons**, ready for delivery to your nearest supermarket.

fairy bread

VOILA!

3 Whipped Cream Science

Cream in Milk

Cream is the fatty part of milk that can be removed before milk is processed. Milk is a nutritious liquid food with many essential nutrients.

4.6% lactose (sugar)
3% other (e.g. minerals and enzymes)
3.2% protein
3.9% milk fat
87.3% water

A pie graph shows the main components of milk.

LACTOSE IN CREAM

Lactose is a sugar that is found in dairy products, such as milk and cream.

LACTOSE INTOLERANCE

Some people are "lactose intolerant", which means that they are not capable of, or have trouble with, digesting the lactose in dairy products.

What's Inside Cream?

First, we need to know about the unseen structure of cream that helps it to turn from a runny liquid into a solid that has a thick, fluffy consistency. Whipping cream contains fat globules floating in an air-bubble structure, also known as an emulsion.

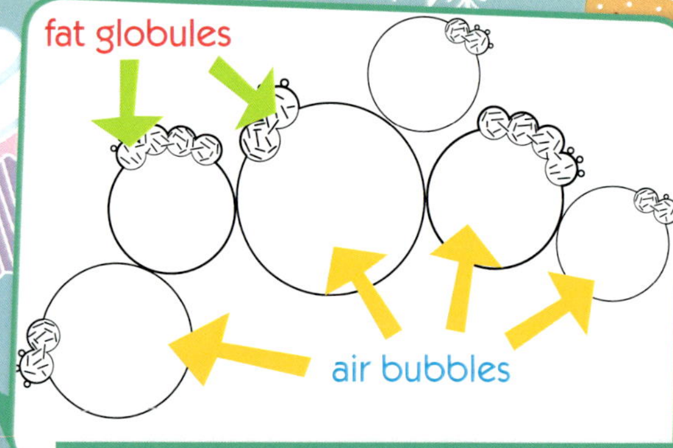

This diagram shows what is happening to the cream structure as it is being whipped – the fat globules start attaching to the air bubbles that are created by the whipping action.

CREAM EMULSION

An emulsion includes two or more substances that do not normally mix together. In cream, globules of fat surround air bubbles.

Not all creams are suitable for whipping, so check the cream container's label for cream called "whipping cream" or for cream that has about 30 to 40 per cent fat.

Why Whipping Cream Thickens

Cream can be whipped with an electric beater, a hand beater or a whisk. The beating action of a beater adds more air bubbles to the cream and causes the fat globules and air to "shake". The cream starts to look frothy and light.

Cream can be whipped.

Cream can be whisked.

Continue Whipping

When you continue beating the cream, the beater helps to strip off the protein coating around the fat globules. This process enables the smaller fat globules to join up and make larger fat globules all around the smaller air bubbles. When this natural process happens, the liquid cream takes on a frothy, whipped consistency.

This diagram shows what happens when the cream is whipped. The fat globules attach around the air bubbles that are created by the whipping action.

Stop When Whipped

If you continue to whip the cream after it has stiffened, the air bubbles will collapse and the fat globules will combine to form butter. The light, foamy appearance made possible by the air bubbles will disappear and you will be left with butter and buttermilk.

The cream has been whipped too much and has turned into butter and buttermilk.

Recipe for **Whipped Cream**

Whipping cream is fun, especially when you see it transform its state from a liquid to a delicious, fluffy, creamy mixture. But what is the scientific method behind the transformation?

Transforming Liquid Cream

Ingredients

- 1 cup of cold, fresh whipping cream
- 1 tablespoon of sugar
- ½ teaspoon of vanilla essence

Equipment

- A cold glass bowl
- An electric beater or a hand-held beater

Science Tip

Only cold cream can be successfully whipped.

COLD GLOBULES OF FAT

There are crystals inside the cream's fat globules. When these crystals are cold, the fat globules and the air can combine to make the whipped cream texture.

cream in its liquid state

cream in its whipped, solid state

Method

1. Pour cold cream into the cold glass bowl.

Science Tip

If you stop beating the cream before it gets thicker, it will return to its original liquid state.

2. Beat the cream on a medium speed for about five minutes until it starts to change into a smooth, thick texture.

3. Stop beating the cream.

Science Tip

If you beat the cream for too long, it becomes warm and the cream will thicken quickly into butter!

4. Add the sugar and the vanilla essence.

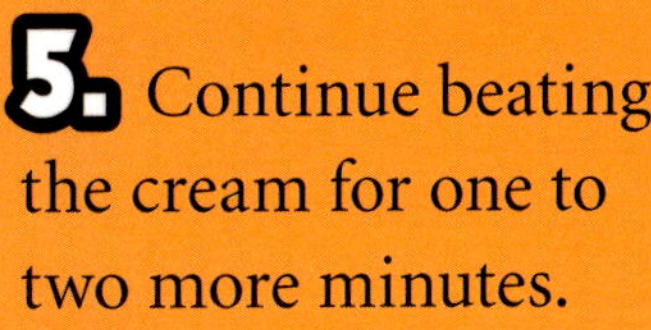

5. Continue beating the cream for one to two more minutes.

6. Stop beating the cream.

4 Science of Dessert Jelly

Jelly **Is a** Joy

Making dessert jelly is quick and easy. But what's really going on as the jelly crystals dissolve in hot water and as it slowly sets into a wobbly solid called jelly?

Jelly's Main Ingredient: Gelatine

Gelatine is made by boiling ground-up animal parts, such as bones and skin. The jelly-like layer at the top of this mixture is gelatine. It has been used since ancient times as a glue and in cooking, and more recently in food, cosmetics, pharmaceuticals and photography.

GELATINE IN JELLY

Gelatine in jelly crystals has been processed to a powder.

cooking with gelatine

Social Studies

Inventor of Gelatine

In 1845, Peter Cooper, a US inventor, first patented powdered gelatine. His patent was for the manufacture of gelatine by drying gelatine then grinding it into a powder.

Peter Cooper

THE FIRST JELLY

In 1897, the first commercially made dessert jelly was made in the USA, but it took several years before it became popular.

A Microscopic View of Jelly

A microscopic view of gelatine shows that it is made up of many long, twisted protein chains that are held together by weak bonds. When hot water is added to a bowl containing the jelly's flavoured gelatine crystals, the weak bonds break apart. This causes the long protein chains in the gelatine to break up into shorter protein chains.

shorter protein chains in hot jelly mixture

long, twisted protein chains in cold, set jelly

What Happens When Jelly Cools and Sets?

When cold water is added and the cooler jelly liquid sets in the fridge, the short protein chains reform as longer protein chains. The combination of water and gelatine crystals prevents the cooler liquid turning into a solid. Instead, the jelly sets into a semi-solid state and wobbles when touched.

Protein chains lengthen as the hot jelly mixture cools down and sets.

Making **Jelly**

Making jelly with jelly crystals and hot water is easy and fun. Once the jelly crystals have dissolved, choose some strong glass dishes or moulds that would be fun to eat out of when the jelly has set.

1. Add Jelly Crystals

Add the whole sachet of jelly crystals to a strong glass bowl that can withstand hot liquids.

2. Add Hot Water

Add about one cup of hot water to the jelly crystals.

3. Stir the Jelly

Stir until the jelly crystals dissolve.

4. Check if Dissolved

Look closely to ensure that the jelly crystals have dissolved.

5. Add Cold Water

Add about half a cup of cold water to the jelly.

6. Pour into Moulds

Pour cooled jelly into glass dishes or moulds.

7. Set, Ready, Eat!

After at least four hours in the fridge, the jelly is ready to eat!

Turkish Delight

Turkish delight is a jelly covered in a fine icing sugar powder. This ancient sweet was created over two hundred years ago.

Turkish delight

Jelly Beans

Turkish delight may have inspired the creation of jelly beans. In 1861, they were made and provided to soldiers during the American Civil War.

jelly beans

Peanut Butter and Jelly Sandwiches

In the USA, the word "jelly" refers to jam. Peanut butter and jelly sandwiches are popular in the USA. American soldiers ate the sandwiches during World War Two and since that time they have been very popular.

making a peanut butter and jelly sandwich

5 Science of Soft Drinks

TEXT TYPE
Information Report
PAGES 18–21

Carbonated soft drinks are made with carbonated water. The first bottled carbonated water was sold in 1835 in the USA as a health drink. Makers then started adding sugar and flavours to create carbonated soft drinks. By 1886, Coca-Cola had been invented by a US pharmacist named Dr John Pemberton. Since then, it has become the bestselling soft drink in the world. The widespread consumption of soft drinks in more recent times has led to health problems in many communities.

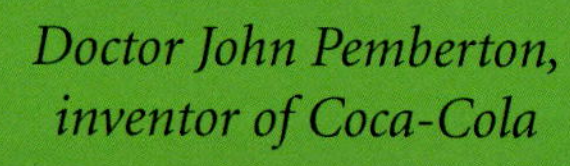

Doctor John Pemberton, inventor of Coca-Cola

ALUMINIUM CANS

Soft drinks were first sold in glass bottles. In 1957, soft drinks became available in aluminium cans.

Processing Carbonated Soft Drinks

Carbonated soft drinks are processed in factories. Water is infused with carbon dioxide, which creates the bubbles. Additives are included to sweeten, flavour, preserve and colour soft drinks. Some soft drinks also contain fruit juice or caffeine. The most commonly used sweetening agents are natural and artificial sugars, in the forms of:

- **sucrose**, which is commonly available as table sugar, and comes from sugar cane and sugar beet
- **fructose**, in the form of high-fructose corn syrup, which is a fruit-based sugar that comes from corn
- **sugar substitutes**, which are used in diet drinks because they have a similar taste to sugar but have little food energy.

TEXT TYPE
Information Report
PAGES 18–21

Sugar

Sugar is a carbohydrate and provides energy. Regular soft drinks contain a lot of added sugar. For example, a 600-millilitre bottle of soft drink contains about 17 teaspoons of sugar. This is about ten teaspoons more added sugar than nutritionists recommend people should have each day.

Over the years, more and more people have regularly consumed soft drinks because they like the sweet taste, the range of flavours and the bubbles. However, the popularity of soft drinks in recent times has led food scientists, nutritionists and medical specialists to observe an increase in health problems. Most of these problems are related to the over-consumption of sugar, namely:

Tooth decay – high levels of sugar promote tooth decay

Obesity – excess sugar is stored in the body as fat

Diabetes – high levels of sugar can lead to diabetes

Immunity – too much processed sugar can cause an increase in insulin in the body. Too much insulin can affect the body's immunity, or the ability to fight disease.

A regular visit to the dentist is ideal.

Carbonated Soft Drinks

Carbonated soft drinks have become so popular that some people drink them instead of water. They do not realise that drinking lots of soft drink increases their sugar consumption and their risk of having health problems. To combat this, it is important that people maintain a healthy diet by limiting their sugar intake, which includes restricting soft drinks so that they are consumed as treats rather than as everyday drinks.

CALCIUM LOSS

Some carbonated soft drinks contain an acid that can contribute to a loss of calcium. People need calcium to build strong bones.

bottles on the production line at a factory

Full cream milk is a good source of calcium.

HEALTH BENEFITS OF WATER

Water makes up about 60 per cent of the body's weight. Depending on size, climate and activity levels, about two to three litres of water should be consumed each day to stay healthy.

Do you like to drink water?

6 Good Sugar or Bad Sugar?

Natural Sugar Foods

Fruits, vegetables and milk are foods that contain natural sugar. Nutritionists suggest that people consume moderate amounts of natural sugar foods because these foods also contain many nutrients, such as vitamins, minerals and fibre.

Eat fruits of all colours.

A variety of vegetables helps to keep us healthy.

Health

Alternatives to Sugar

Stevia is a natural sugar processed from a sweet-tasting herb.

Xylitol is found in the fibres of fruits and vegetables. Both stevia and xylitol have fewer calories than sugar from sugar cane.

stevia leaves

Added Sugar in Processed Food and Drinks

Nutritionists and doctors caution people not to consume too many processed foods and drinks that have high levels of added sugar. It is recommended that people only consume about six to eight teaspoons of added sugar every day.

a sugar cube

A **Suggested** Natural **Sugar** Plan

In Australia, it is recommended that children consume about 80 to 90 grams of natural sugar each day. Natural sugar occurs in many foods, such as fruit, vegetables, milk and milk products. Here are just some of them.

A medium-sized apple = **20 grams**

A medium-sized banana = **17 grams**

Half a cup of strawberries = **5 grams**

One teaspoon of honey = **7 grams**

A medium-sized orange = **19 grams**

Half a cup of plain yoghurt = **9 grams**

A glass of milk = **13 grams**

Yoghurt and milk are high-calcium foods.

Total = 90 grams natural sugar for one day

Note: All measurements are approximate and refer to the amount of natural sugar in these foods. The amount can vary depending on the size of the fruit or serving. There are higher levels of natural sugar in very ripe and naturally sweet fruits.

Vegetables: Eat a variety of raw and cooked vegetables daily (e.g. peas, carrots, sweet potato and beetroot) because their natural sugar content is healthy for you.

7 Crispy, Chocolate Chip Cookie Science

Do you like a thin, crispy cookie or a thick, chewy cookie? Cooking is a scientific process that can be varied to change the result, depending on your preference. There are tips in the recipe below.

Choc-Nut-Chip Cookies

This recipe will make about 24 thin, crispy Choc-Nut-Chip cookies. But if you want to bake cookies with a thicker, chewier consistency, make changes to the recipe by following the tips in the science fact boxes.

Dry Ingredients

- 2 ¼ cups plain **flour**
- 1 teaspoon **baking powder**
- 1 cup white sugar
- ½ cup **brown sugar**

Liquid Ingredients

- 1 **egg**
- ¼ cup milk
- 1 teaspoon vanilla extract

Science Fact: Flour

Replace flour with bread flour to make chewier cookies.

Science Fact: Baking Powder

Baking powder is a raising agent that causes a chemical reaction, in which carbon dioxide gas is released into the cookie mixture. This process helps the mixture to rise and spread during baking.

Make a flatter cookie, by adding a little more baking powder.

Science Fact: Brown Sugar

Extra brown sugar helps to make chewier cookies. The moisture in brown sugar creates a chewier texture.

Science Fact: Egg

Replace egg with two yolks to make chewier cookies.

Other Ingredients

- 225 grams **butter** (room temperature)
- 1 ¾ cups chocolate chips
- ¼ cup chopped walnuts or peanuts

Science Fact: Butter

Melt the butter to make chewier cookies.

Equipment

- *one small bowl*
- *one medium-sized bowl*
- *one large bowl*
- *a whisk*
- *a knife*
- *one tablespoon*
- *a wooden spoon or a spatula*
- *a chopping board*
- *a hand-held electric beater*
- *enough baking paper to cover the tray*
- *an oven tray*
- *a sifter*

Preparation

- Pre-heat the oven to 190 degrees Celsius.
- Cover the oven tray with baking paper.
- Take the butter out of the fridge to soften.

The Method

1. Sift Some Dry Ingredients

Sift the flour and baking powder in the medium-sized bowl.

2. Whisk the Liquid Ingredients

Whisk the egg, milk and vanilla extract in the small bowl.

3. Mix the Butter and Sugar

Use the knife to cut the butter into tiny cubes on the chopping board.

Science Fact: Beat

The beating action adds air to the mixture.

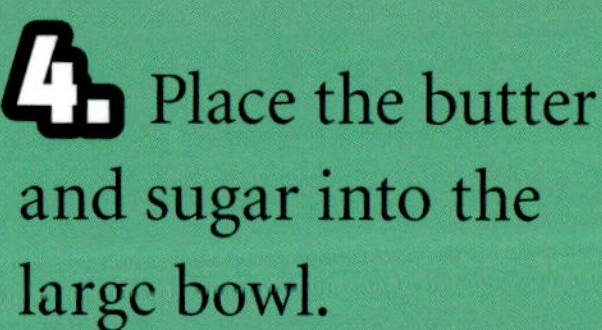

4. Place the butter and sugar into the large bowl.

5. Use the hand-held electric beater to **beat** the sugar and butter slowly. Then increase the speed until the mixture is creamy. Turn off the electric beater.

Combine all the Ingredients

6. Add the whisked ingredients to the sugar and butter. Use the electric beater to mix until the ingredients are completely blended. Turn off the electric beater.

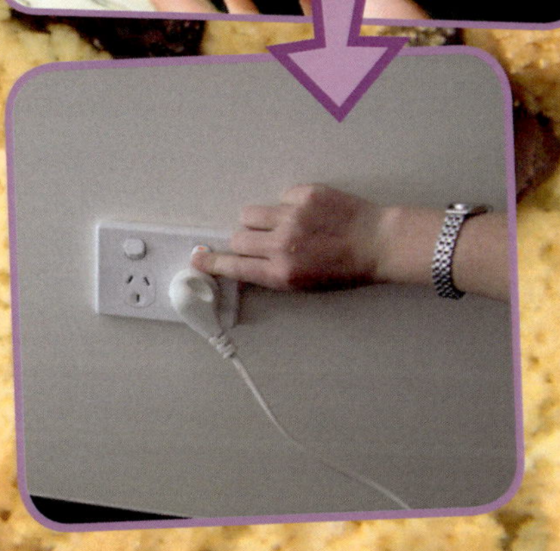

7. Add the **dry** ingredients to the mixture. Use the wooden spoon or a spatula to mix all the ingredients thoroughly.

Science Fact: Dry

If you are baking in a hot, humid climate, add more dry ingredients, such as a ¼ cup of flour.

8. Add the chocolate chips and chopped walnuts (or peanuts) to the mixture. Use the wooden spoon to mix all the ingredients thoroughly.

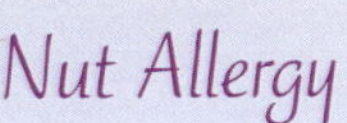

Nut Allergy

For people with nut allergies, leave out the nuts and add a quarter of a cup of chocolate chips.

The Final Stages of the Recipe

9. Make Cookie Shapes

Use a tablespoon to scoop out a spoonful of the mixture and put it into the palm of your hand. Use both hands to roll it into a ball and then place it on the tray covered with baking paper. Use a fork or your fingers to pat the ball down to about a one-centimetre thickness.

Each ball of cookie **dough** should be the same size. Leave enough space between the cookies for them to spread out when baking.

Science Fact: Dough

Chill the dough in the fridge for 15 minutes to make chewier cookies.

10. Put in the Oven

Ask an adult to help you place the tray into the oven. After ten minutes, quickly check the cookies through the glass window in the oven door. They may only need two to three more minutes to finish baking.

11. Take out of the Oven

Ask an adult to remove the tray from the oven. Leave the cookies to cool on the tray for about five minutes before you carefully place them on a wire tray to cool down completely.

8 Creative Food Chemistry

Food chemistry is an exciting subject that chefs use to help them create recipes. Chefs learn about the chemical reactions that happen when ingredients are mixed and cooked.

Many restaurant kitchens include equipment adapted from science laboratories.

Edible Food Art

Chefs who want to create edible food art must understand hydrocolloids in order to create amazing dishes. Hydrocolloids come from natural sources that have been used in traditional cooking for many years.

Chemistry

Hydrocolloids

Hydrocolloids are substances that form a gel when mixed with water; for example, gelatine, which is used to set jelly. Other common hydrocolloids are flour and cornflour.

Seaweed Hydrocolloids

One hydrocolloid that is made from seaweed is called agar-agar. If a natural flavour, like vanilla essence, and gelatine are added to agar-agar, the chef can make thin, transparent gel sheets. The hydrocolloid sheets won't split when placed or moulded over certain foods.

making a cylinder shape out of caramel made with olive oil and a sugar substitute called isomalt

CHEF FEATURE

Ferran Adrià

A **Chef** of **Edible** Art

Ferran Adrià has been voted the world's best chef. His restaurant in Roses, Spain, is so popular that two million people try to get a booking but only 8000 people are successful.

Ferran Adrià

Ferran Adrià's restaurant, El Bulli

What's **on the Menu?**

Over the years, Ferran Adrià has created amazing edible art. These dishes are enjoyed by the lucky people who manage to reserve a table one year in advance!

staff meeting at El Bulli

Some Favourite Dishes

Entree

Brick Pastry and Lemon Parmesan Skeins (2001)

Bread and Pine Nut Scarves (2003)

Main Course

Duckling with Seaweed Salt and Vegetable Scallops (1999)

Dessert

Pea Jelly with Banana and Lime Ice-Cream (2005)

Petits Fours

Chocolate Lollies with Pumpkin Seeds *Croquant* (2001)

The year in brackets denotes when the dish was first created in the El Bulli restaurant by Ferran Adrià.

a tantalising starter

a frozen cocktail made with salty air, served in an ice cube

langoustine with quinoa

Index

Glossary

buttermilk The liquid that is left behind after butter is separated from cream or milk

carbohydrate A compound of carbon, hydrogen and oxygen, such as starch or sugar, that provides energy when eaten

diabetes A disease caused by having abnormal amounts of insulin in the body and therefore too much sugar in the blood

edible art Delicious food that is presented in a unique and beautiful way

insulin A chemical produced in the body that controls how much sugar is in the blood

milk solids The substance that remains when the water is removed from milk; it contains protein, fat, lactose and minerals

nutritionist Someone who studies food and nutrition, and helps people to choose the right quantities of food that is good for them in order to be healthy

protein A substance necessary for good health and growth, which is found in foods such as meat, milk, eggs, nuts and beans